Summer Sunshine

With sparkly wishes for my god-daughter, Daisy Brett
Love Emma

First published in Great Britain in 2006 by Hodder Children's Books

5

A Catalogue record for this book is available from the British Library.

ISBN: 978 0 340 91195 2

Printed and bound in China.

The paper and board used in this paperback by Hodder Children's Books are natural recyclable products made from wood grown in sustainable forests. The manufacturing processes conform to the environmental regulations of the country of origin.

Hodder Children's Books
A division of Hachette Children's Books, 338 Euston Road, London NW1 3BH
An Hachette Livre UK Company

Summer Sunshine

and other stories

A division of Hachette Children's Books

How to make your Felicity wishes

WISH

With this book comes an extra special wish
for you and your best friend.
Hold the book together at each end and
both close your eyes.
Wriggle your noses and think of a
number under ten.
Open your eyes, whisper the numbers you
thought of to each other.
Add these numbers together. This is your

Magic Number.

you

best friend

Place your little finger
on the stars, and say your magic number
out loud together. Now make your wish
quietly to yourselves. And maybe, one day,
your wish might just come true.

Love Felicity

Contents

Summer Sunshine

Summer Sunshine

Felicity and her best friends, Holly, Polly, Daisy and Winnie, were beside themselves with excitement. Despite being squashed uncomfortably beneath enormous heavy backpacks, their fairy wings quivered with anticipation.

"I've been looking forward to this day for so long!" squealed Felicity as she landed beside her friends in the train station with a fairylike thud.

"I never thought it would actually arrive," said Winnie excitedly. "And now it has, I can hardly believe it!"

Winnie was at school with Felicity, Holly, Polly and Daisy. She wanted to be an Adventure Fairy when she graduated. It had been her idea, one lunchtime, that they all go inter-railing around Fairy World together that summer.

At first Daisy wasn't very keen. She loved her home more than anything and never ventured far from it. The flowers in her garden needed constant care and attention.

Holly had been equally sceptical. She prided herself on being the most fashionable fairy in Little Blossoming but in the big, wide, Fairy World, Holly was worried that she wouldn't stand out.

"I think it will be fun!" said Polly, encouraging her friends. "Just think of all the amazing places that we'll be able to see for real, instead of in a geography textbook."

"A whole month of new experiences and adventures!" cried Winnie, bouncing up and down.

"And memories that will stay with us for ever!" added Felicity dreamily.

* * *

"Has everyone got their tickets?" asked Winnie, taking charge.

"Yes!" chorused Holly, Polly, and Daisy, waggling them in the air.

"I think so!" flapped Felicity, frantically unzipping every pocket on her rucksack. "Oh, no!" she muttered hastily under her breath.

"Um... Felicity!" said Polly, trying to get her friend's attention.

"Hold on a second," said Felicity, getting more flustered by the minute as every pocket she emptied revealed no ticket.

Polly, Holly, Daisy and Winnie stared in amazement as Felicity rummaged through the most bizarre items they had ever seen packed in a suitcase! Four bags of strawberry fizzy laces, a bird bath, two mobile phones (just in case she lost one and couldn't speak to her friends), ten pairs of stripy tights and a dozen sparkle bars!

"Felicity!" said Polly sternly, trying to get her attention. "Look!"

Felicity stopped and looked up at Polly, who was waving two tickets.

"You gave me your ticket to look after... remember!"

Felicity flushed bright pink. She was notorious for forgetting things,

especially when they were important.

* * *

With their tickets stamped and their bags carefully stowed away in the overhead shelves, the five fairy friends settled down for the exciting journey ahead.

"I hope no one else joins us!" said Holly, lounging luxuriously across the spare seat next to her.

Just then the compartment door swung open.

"Hello!" said a little voice. "Is this carriage number 57?"

Holly quickly jumped up. "Um, yes, yes. Is this your seat? I was just, um, keeping it warm for you," she said as she slid over to her own seat, her cheeks a little flushed.

"Hello!" said Felicity, excited to meet a new friend. "I'm Felicity and these are my best friends, Holly, Polly, Daisy and Winnie. We're going on a backpacking holiday around Fairy World. We're going to Bird Island via Dreamland. There are so many places to visit, and so little time. Where are you going?"

To Felicity's amazement, the little fairy said nothing in return. Felicity watched as she started to unpack a book from her bag, kick off her shoes and curl up in her seat. It wasn't

until the little fairy reached into her bag and pulled out Suzi Sparkle's latest CD that Felicity realized she was listening to a CD player and hadn't heard anything Felicity had said!

"Oh, well, there's plenty of time to make friends during the journey," thought Felicity to herself, dying to know more about the fairy in their compartment.

* * *

As the train slowly fluttered out of Little Blossoming, the fairies left behind the billowing green hills and were soon soaring past long golden beaches, magnificent valleys and breathtaking forests.

"The view is incredible!" said Holly, mesmerized by the changing landscape.

"Just amazing," said Felicity, feeling the chug-chug of the train rocking against her tired wings.

"I'm exhausted," yawned Polly, "and we haven't even been anywhere yet!"

The excitement of the trip had drained each of the fairy friends. Ever so slowly, as every mile passed, the fairies grew sleepier and sleepier, until at last the only one who was awake was the little fairy listening to music in the corner.

* * *

"Um, hello! Hello! Wake up! Is this your stop?" said the little fairy, rustling Felicity's hair with her wand. "Hello! Yoooohoooo! If you don't wake up now I'm afraid you're going to miss your stop!" she said more loudly.

Suddenly, thinking she was in bed, Felicity rolled over and fell off her seat.

"Wha…Where am I?" she burst out, noisily enough to wake all the others.

"It's the next stop," said the fairy. "Do you have to get off here?"

Winnie was as muddled as Felicity and had no idea how long they had all been asleep for, or where in Fairy World they were.

"Quickly, everyone!" said Winnie, taking charge. "Pack up your things; we only have a few moments to get out of here before the train pulls away!"

Holly, Polly, Daisy, Felicity and Winnie flew madly about the carriage, gathering their belongings.

"My wand!" burst out Felicity. "I can't find my wand!"

"Leave it!" cried Winnie. "We have

to change trains or we won't make the connection! Any moment now the train is going to pull aw—" And just as Winnie was starting to say "away", the slow roll of the train's wheels began to move underneath them.

Distraught, the five fairy friends pressed their noses up against the glass to watch in desperation as the station platform passed by.

"That platform sign says Bloomfield," said Holly, staring quizzically at the sign in the distance. "I didn't think we had to change trains until Sweet Hill."

Everyone looked at Winnie, who looked at the tickets and then at the little fairy that had woken them up from their sleep.

"You've only been asleep for half an hour. Sweet Hill is where I'm going too, but it's not for another..." and she looked at her watch, "... fourteen hours!"

Felicity, Holly, Polly and Daisy groaned, dropped their bags and slumped back into their seats.

* * *

Feeling a little better for their nap and relieved by their close escape, the fairy friends were in high spirits once more.

"My name's Felicity and this is Holly, Polly, Daisy and Winnie," said Felicity, tapping each of her fairy friends on their knee with her wand.

"And I'm Kristen," said the fairy as she took off her headphones. "I'm sorry if I seemed a little rude earlier, but I've just been given a copy of Suzi Sparkle's latest album and I was dying to listen to it."

"No, not at all," said Felicity, relieved that the fairy hadn't been ignoring them on purpose. "We all love Suzi Sparkle too."

"Why are you going to Sweet Hill?" asked Winnie. "Are you going on holiday too?"

"Oh, no," said Kristen. "I've just had my holiday in Little Blossoming, and now I'm going home!"

All five fairy friends giggled!

"How funny," burst out Felicity. "We're almost doing the same thing, only in the opposite direction!"

"We're not staying in Sweet Hill though," said Polly. "We're just changing trains there. We're on our way to Bird Island via Dreamland."

"Oh, I've always wanted to go to Bird Island," said Kristen. "It's supposed to be beautiful! I've heard that every morning at sunrise, all the birds on the island wake up and sing a song that's so moving it will bring tears to your eyes."

"Wow! It sounds amazing," said Daisy and Polly together.

Felicity and Holly shot each other a distraught look. Felicity wasn't one for early mornings and Holly liked her beauty sleep, so the thought of being woken up early every morning was not their idea of a holiday!

"Well," said Polly, "we've got fourteen hours to go even before we get to Sweet Hill. Why don't we play some games to entertain ourselves?" she suggested, and looked around for inspiration. Suddenly she spotted an old discarded newspaper and gave each fairy a double-page sheet. "Best outfit wins!"

Polly immediately set to work making a hat. She'd learnt how to fold paper in an origami book from the library. Holly based her outfit on a pattern she had seen in the latest edition of *Fairy Girl*. Felicity and

Daisy made skirts decorated with newspaper flowers and Winnie and Kristen decided to make a dress to fit both of them!

When the ticket inspector knocked on the carriage door all she could see was a sea of rustling paper pages in front of her eyes.

"Hmm, I'll come back later," she said, completely baffled.

The fairy friends couldn't control their giggles and rolled around the carriage floor in fits of laughter.

* * *

The rest of the journey was more fun than any of the fairies could have imagined. Felicity had expected the destination to be the exciting part of the journey and getting there the boring bit. But the journey was turning out every bit as fun.

"There's no going to sleep!" announced their new friend Kristen when she saw Holly and Polly yawn in unison. "I have to get off at 3 a.m. and you have to change then too! If we miss our stop, I'll never get home and you won't reach your holiday destination!"

So the fairy friends played games, told silly jokes and stories late into

the night. Kristen told them all about her home, Sweet Hill. The fairy friends gasped in amazement as they tried to imagine houses that float on fluffy white clouds, a theme park where all your dreams come true, magical castles and, most importantly, the world-famous Sweet Hill Ice Cream Emporium.

For the tenth time that night, the fairies played I Spy.

"I spy with my little eye..." began Winnie, "something beginning with 'T'."

"Train?" guessed Polly.

Winnie shook her head.

"Tiara?" Daisy pointed at the open rucksack.

"Nope," said Winnie.

"Tights?" asked Kristen.

"No!" giggled Winnie.

"Give us a clue!" squealed Holly.

Winnie pointed to Kristen's watch.

"Watch!" shouted Felicity triumphantly.

"NO!" said Winnie, exasperated. "That doesn't begin with 'T'! It's 'time'."

"Time?" said Polly.

"Yes!" said Winnie. "It's time to get our things together because we arrive at Sweet Hill in less than ten minutes!"

* * *

When the train drew into Sweet Hill station the fairies had packed up their things and were busy swapping addresses and phone numbers with Kristen. They were all a little upset at saying goodbye and each made a secret wish that Kristen could come with them.

"If ever you find yourselves in Sweet Hill again, you must come and stay!" urged Kristen, who was also secretly wishing she could continue with her new friends to Bird Island. "Keep in touch!" she cried as she slowly walked away.

"Wait!" said Felicity, running after her. "You've forgotten this!" And she put the newspaper hat over Kristen's crown to remember them by.

"Right," said Winnie, getting her bearings. "Our connecting train leaves from platform five, so that should be us over there." And she pointed to a bright-red speed train with a large pair of wings on the sides of the engine.

When they reached the train, they found a ticket-inspector fairy blocking the way.

"Please accept our sincere apologies," she said, "but I'm afraid this train has broken down. The repair fairies won't be available to fix it until first thing tomorrow morning. I suggest you find something to amuse yourselves until then."

Felicity and her friends groaned.

"What are we going to do?" asked Holly, starting to panic. "It's 3 a.m. – nowhere will be open!"

"We could phone Kristen," said Felicity, suddenly perking up.

"Felicity, I think Kristen's probably climbing into her bed as we speak!" said Polly sensibly.

Felicity's heart sank. She'd been looking forward to seeing her new friend again.

"Then why don't we visit that all-night Ice Cream Emporium Kristen told us about?" said Daisy.

Suddenly Felicity perked up. She had been dreaming about super-puff berry sherbet ever since Kristen had told her about it.

* * *

The streets of Sweet Hill were magical. Morning dew settled on golden cobblestones that glittered in the lamplight. As far as the eye could see, magnificent houses floated softly on fluffy white clouds.

"I feel like I'm in a dream," said Daisy.

"I feel as though I've been here before!" said Felicity, looking around in awe. "Kristen described it all so wonderfully. It's just as I imagined."

"What an adventure!" said Winnie. She leapt into the air to do a loop-the-loop.

When the fairy friends turned the next corner, Sweet Hill Ice Cream Emporium lay before them. A warm yellow light flooded out on to the street and dozens of fairies sat with ice creams that boasted more different-coloured scoops than Felicity and her friends had ever seen.

SWEET HILL
ICE CREAM EMPORIUM

Within moments they were inside and ordering scrumptious double helpings of the weirdest and most wonderful flavours they could ever imagine.

"I'd like a scoop of super-puff berry sherbet," said Felicity excitedly to the waitress fairy behind the counter. "A friend told me it was the best."

The waitress looked awkward. "I'm very sorry," she said. "But I've just given the last scoop to that fairy over there," and she pointed in the direction of a booth in the corner.

Felicity couldn't believe her eyes. It was Kristen!

"Guess who!" said Felicity, sneaking up behind Kristen and covering her eyes.

Kristen spun round and nearly fell off her stool!

"Felicity!" she cried, flinging her arms around her new friend. "What are you doing here?"

"We've come to persuade you to come with us to Bird Island!" joked Felicity.

"Oh, you don't need to persuade me!" said Kristen, laughing. "After I left you I enquired about tickets and they said that owing to a faulty train there were dozens of spare seats available on the first train tomorrow morning! There was no point in going to bed, so I thought I'd come here until it was time."

Felicity couldn't believe her ears!

"But it's our connecting train that's broken down! Now we can all go to Bird Island together!"

It was only the start of their summer adventure, but already each of the fairies' secret wishes had come true.

No matter how small or big, follow your dreams wherever they take you

Fairy Friends

Fairy Friends

Felicity, Holly, Polly, Winnie and Daisy and their new friend Kristen were on their summer adventure, travelling around Fairy World together.

The steady rocking of their train had them nodding off within seconds. It had been a long night. The train to Bird Island via Dreamland had been delayed at Sweet Hill, but now they were finally on their way.

* * *

At midday Daisy woke up with a start.

"What was that?" she said, pinging out of her seat.

"Wha...What?" stammered Holly, rubbing her eyes and adjusting her crown.

"It sounded like a monster!" Polly's voice was shaking.

"You're imagining things!" said Holly.

"No! I heard it too!" cried Kristen. "I thought I was dreaming!"

"GGGGGGgggggrrrrrrrrr!" came the noise again, so loudly this time that it made Daisy's wand jiggle.

"Felicity!" squealed Holly, shaking her friend's shoulder.

Slowly Felicity opened her eyes, confused to find all her fairy friends gathered around her, staring at her tummy.

"I think your stomach is telling us it's lunchtime!" giggled Polly.

* * *

The buffet car in the train was the most glamorous the fairies had ever seen.

"Gosh!" said Holly, looking at the tables with their white linen table-cloths and silver teapots. "You don't get this on the trains in Little Blossoming!"

"Nor in Sweet Hill," said Kristen.

The fairy waitress came towards them, smiling. "We're really full, so I'm afraid you'll have to wait," she said, "unless you wouldn't mind sharing a table?"

Felicity's tummy rumbled its most enormous rumble yet.

"I think we'll share," said Holly urgently.

* * *

The fairies at the table they joined had almost finished their pudding and were huddled deep in conversation, in a language that the fairy friends had never heard before.

Felicity smiled and waved her wand in a friendly hello.

Frowning, the foreign fairies stopped talking, picked up their wands and one by one handed them over to Felicity!

"No no!" said Felicity, passing them back. "I was just saying 'hello'! I don't want your wands!"

"H-e-l-l-o," said Holly loudly.

"They're foreign, not deaf, Holly!" said Polly, laughing.

The foreign fairies got up and stood facing Felicity and her friends. Gravely they raised their right arms, spread the fingers on their right hands, placed their thumbs on their noses and in unison blew a raspberry!

"Well, how rude!" said Holly, aghast. "If they don't want us to share their table, they only have to say!"

“Is there a problem here?” said the waitress fairy, arriving just at the right time. “I see the fairies from Dreamland have welcomed you in their traditional way.”

“Traditional way?” laughed Polly, who was frantically rummaging for her phrase book.

“And it’s customary,” said the waitress, “to reply with a similar gesture!”

* * *

After their initial sticky start the fairies sat down to enjoy a meal together. Armed only with Polly’s book they were able to discover that the Dreamland fairies were on their way home. Their names were Schubi, Blina and Lishu. At least, that’s what Polly thought their names were. Felicity was of the mind that Polly might have it wrong… and

that these were actually their favourite colours!

"Fancy eating your meal back to front like that!" said Holly, watching the Dreamland fairies tucking into their main course after finishing their pudding.

"I think it's very sensible," said Daisy. "If you eat your pudding first, you'll always have room for it – and puddings are the nicest bit of any meal!"

* * *

"It says here," said Polly, consulting her phrase book, "that in Dreamland anything you've ever dreamed of can happen for real!"

"What an incredible place," said Felicity, thinking of all the dreams that she'd love to come true. "If only it wasn't just a stopover and we had

arranged to spend more time there on our way to Bird Island."

"Well, we could try to ask our new friends where the best place to stay is, so that we make the most of our trip," suggested Polly. She leafed to the back of her phrase book.

"Ahem," said Polly. She cleared her throat to get the Dreamland fairies' attention.

Lishu got up, clapped her hands excitedly, put her hand in her pocket and handed Polly a cough sweet.

"Ta chukka," said Polly, bemused. This isn't going to be easy, she thought. "Liff ena hise?" she said stiffly. She had no idea whether she had the pronunciation right.

Lishu, Blina and Schubi beamed their biggest smiles.

"Ohyi, de en hugh gesten hise wott inde plas cool 'Daydreams'."

"What did you ask? What did she say?" said Felicity, bouncing up and down and looking expectantly at Polly.

"I asked them where they live," said Polly proudly, "but I haven't a clue what they said back!" She began frantically flicking through her book.

"I'm sure I heard her say the word 'Daydreams' at the end – that's Dreamland's capital city, isn't it?" said Daisy. "It would be perfect if that is where they're from, because that's where we're planning to visit."

"Ask them where we can stay!" urged Felicity.

Polly braced herself, smiled at the three foreign fairies and said, "Ugo tta rooo men?"

"Ohyi, ohyi," they said in unison.

"Ugo tta beein liff en wid duss forum edda," said Schubi, with nods of approval from all her friends.

"Ohyi, forum edda. Itum ma kenn ussen delli rear ee oushly hap pi," said Blina, tears welling up in her eyes.

"What was that?" said Felicity "Are you sure you asked the right question? Blina looks like she's going to cry!"

Anxious to look like she knew what was going on, Polly made a wild and almost correct guess.

"Oh, yes," she said confidently. "I asked them where we could stay and they said that the best place to stay was a hotel called 'Wid Duss' in Forum Edda."

"Forum Edda," said Felicity dreamily.

"It does sound like somewhere you'd see in dream."

"The words actually mean 'for ever'," said Polly, consulting her book. "You're right, it does sound dreamy."

* * *

For the rest of their journey the new fairy friends didn't leave the buffet car. Felicity laughed so hard that afternoon that her cheeks ached. They discovered that the best way to communicate was by drawing... but none of them was very good at it!

Holly learnt how to make a 'Dreamland wish' by closing her eyes as though she was asleep and wiggling her wand with a snore!

Kristen and Daisy bravely tried some of Lishu's biscuits. They looked like they were made of mud, but tasted delicious.

And Blina tried desperately to teach them all how to sing the Dreamland national anthem, which sounded to Felicity as if it was completely out of tune… but then, Felicity had never got top marks in music!

* * *

At last an announcement was made over the loudspeakers that Dreamland was only fifteen minutes away.

"I can't wait to see for real all those places Lishu, Blina and Schubi have told us about in pictures," said Holly, heaving on her rucksack.

"I hope it looks better than it does in their pictures!" giggled Kristen.

"Forum Edda looked very close to where they live on the map," said Daisy. "I hope Hotel Wid Duss is what I'm dreaming of!"

* * *

When Felicity, Holly, Polly, Winnie, Daisy and Kristen stepped on to the platform to join their new friends, they knew at once they were in Dreamland.

"Birds flying backwards!" gasped Felicity, as she pointed up to the sky.

"A café on a cloud!" squealed Polly, opening her eyes wide.

"You're never going to believe this!" said Holly. She tugged her friends to where Lishu, Schubi and Blina were standing, arms outstretched, trying to hail a taxi.

"Self-driving bicycle taxis with wings!" said Felicity, barely able to grasp what she was seeing.

"I did say," said Polly, "absolutely anything you dream of can come true in Dreamland!"

"I'd like to dream that I'll stay here for ever!" said Felicity in awe. "I think it's the most incredible place I've ever been!"

* * *

But what was truly incredible was yet to come. As the magical bicycle taxis flew into the sky and away from Daydreams train station, the fairies didn't know where to look next.

On one side were houses shaped like lollipops with curly-wurly slides that took you to the ground. On the other was a lake, not full of water, but of fizzy yellow sherbet that glistened in the sun's rays.

"Oh, I hope Hotel Wid Duss isn't far," said Felicity, longing to be close enough to go for a sherbet swim before they left.

"Forum Edda must be soon," said Polly. "I can feel the wheels of the bicycle beginning to dip."

"No, no," said Holly, looking down. "This isn't Hotel Wid Duss, this is their house. I recognize it from the pictures."

* * *

Schubi, Lishu and Blina lived together in a house that didn't look like anything Felicity or her friends had ever seen before. From the outside it

looked like a huge beach ball, covered with windows whose shutters opened to reveal dozens of smiling fairies.

"They live with an awful lot of fairies!" said Felicity, excited at the possibility of making even more friends – with her limited drawing skills!

As the bicycles landed, all the waving fairies rushed down to the main entrance and stood to welcome them with the traditional raspberry greeting. Felicity thought she was going to pass out with giggles!

"Dis isen noo frenden," said Lishu loudly, addressing the crowd. "Holly, Polly, Felicity, Daisy, Winnie an Kristen!" she said, pointing to each of them in turn. "Dey av commen toe liff en wid duss forum edda!"

The whole throng of fairies went wild with cheers and descended on Felicity and her friends in a shower of hugs and kisses, amongst cries of, "Wid duss, forum edda!"

* * *

It was Polly who guessed what had happened first. When one of the fairies whisked away her backpack and she was shown to a beautiful room with everything she had ever dreamed of, her guess was confirmed.

Polly wanted to be a tooth fairy when she graduated from the School of Nine Wishes, and she had always dreamed of a place just perfect for her. A room with pictures of large toothy smiles on the walls, books about teeth and toothy tales on the bookshelf, and a duvet with a picture of her favourite front tooth.

"I don't understand," said Felicity, bursting happily into Polly's room and flinging herself on the toothy duvet. "I thought we were going to stay in Hotel Wid Duss, but I've just been shown to the most beautiful room I could ever have dreamed of. It's got pink curtains, pink carpet, pink wallpaper, pink bedclothes and even a pink light... it's pink heaven!"

Just as Polly picked up her phrase book, Kristen, Daisy, Holly, Lishu, Schubi and Blina all ran into her room.

"I'm afraid there's been a mistake," said Polly earnestly. "There is no hotel 'Wid Duss'."

"That doesn't matter!" said Holly, in ecstasy. "We can stay here! Lishu has just shown me to the most amazing room full of mirrors and make-up. There's even a walk-in wardrobe full of beautiful outfits that are just my size."

Patiently Polly explained. "There is no hotel 'Wid Duss' because 'Wid Duss' actually means 'with us', and as I already said on the train, 'forum edda' isn't a place. It means 'for ever'."

Ever so slowly, what Polly was saying dawned on all the fairy friends.

"So Lishu, Schubi and Blina think that we are going to live 'with them', 'for ever'?" said Felicity. She was quite keen on the idea.

Polly nodded. "Dreams only come true if you believe in them for ever, which means we will never be able to go back to Little Blossoming if we stay here for more than one night."

Felicity sighed and looked across at Lishu, Blina and Schubi, who were anxiously watching their new friends and trying to work out what was going on.

Felicity knew what they had to do. Dreamland was the most amazing place she'd ever seen. But Little Blossoming was their home, and she'd never be able to live anywhere else.

"How are we going to tell them we can't stay with them for ever?" said Daisy, distraught. "They've been so kind to us, and given us such a lovely place to live. Whatever we say will break their hearts!"

"And mine!" said Felicity. She looked at the troubled faces of Lishu, Blina and Schubi, and across the hall to her perfectly dreamy pink bedroom.

"We could just go quietly tomorrow morning without saying anything,"

suggested Holly, who was never very good in awkward situations.

"No," said Felicity. "There has to be another way."

Suddenly, she had an idea. Pulling her notebook and pen from her pocket, Felicity tried very carefully to draw the best drawing she possibly could.

When she showed Lishu, Blina and Schubi their eyes welled up with tears.

They knew that it meant their new fairy friends would not be staying for ever, as they'd hoped, but would be leaving to go to Bird Island in the morning.

But before their fairy tears had rolled down their cheeks, Felicity quickly drew something on the next page that she knew the Dreamland fairies would understand.

Lishu, Blina and Schubi whooped and gave all five fairy friends one enormous hug all at the same time.

"What in Fairy World did you draw?" squealed Holly, her wings crumpling under the hug.

"I drew something that said even though we would have to go, we will never leave this place because we will always return, in our dreams... forum edda!"

And everyone cheered!

Even though everyone seems
different on the outside

we all share the same
dreams and wishes
underneath

Magical Moments

Magical Moments

Felicity, Holly, Polly, Daisy, Winnie and their new friend Kristen were on a holiday that had taken them further away from home than they had ever been before.

With adventure in their hearts, the fairy friends had travelled from Little Blossoming to Sweet Hill where, after a short and unexpected stopover, they

had changed trains to take them to Dreamland. In Dreamland, their dreams had quite literally come true and now, after two days, three hours and forty-five minutes, the five exhausted but very excited fairy friends were almost at their final destination, Bird Island.

Winnie wanted to be an adventure fairy when she graduated from the School of Nine Wishes, and couldn't stop her wings jiggling with anticipation. "I don't know what I'm looking forward to most," said Winnie, clapping her hands excitedly as she jumped down from the train on to the platform.

"I can't wait to see the hotel," said Polly, who had spent days organizing the booking. "It's got a five-wing rating with beautiful sea views!"

"I can't wait to see the beautiful Bird Island flowers," said Daisy dreamily.

"I'm looking forward to the boat ride to the island," said Holly.

"But what about your hair?" said Felicity, knowing that Holly would hate getting her hair wet. "All that sea air will play havoc with your locks!"

"Oh, who cares about hair when there's adventure in the air?" said Holly dramatically.

"Gosh!" said Polly. "You've certainly been bitten by the travel bug! And you were the one who wasn't keen on this trip."

Holly remembered her fears about not being noticed in the big, wide, fashionable Fairy World. "This trip has taught me lots of things," said

Holly earnestly. "Most of all that it doesn't matter what other people think of you as long as you are being true to yourself."

"Yes," agreed Daisy. "I remember I was the same. I didn't want to come at first either because I was scared. But uncertain situations have shown me that I am braver than I thought."

Felicity hugged her friends. "Well," she said, pointing to a rickety boat

that bobbed about in the distant harbour, "I have a feeling there are more uncertain situations to come!"

* * *

The boat was old, very old! When the six fairy friends reached the boat they began to wonder how in Fairy World it was able to float at all.

"Well, hi there!" came a soft, lazy voice from behind the fairy friends. "You the six fairies for the afternoon transfer?"

Felicity, Holly, Polly, Daisy, Winnie and Kristen were dumbstruck. Forgetting their manners, their mouths flopped wide open as they stared at the fairy coming towards them.

* * *

"Sorry about being late," said the fairy, "but this is a sleepy town that only wakes up at night. If I hadn't been taking you across to the birds, I would have snoozed right through till supper."

"Great wings!" was all Holly could say.

"Oh, these?" said the skipper fairy. She had wings so huge they were almost bigger than her! "We've all got these kinda wings here. They double up as a super-large sunshade when it gets too hot."

"I guess we should be going," said Polly, looking at her watch. "The hotel at Bird

Island will be expecting us, and we're already late."

The skipper fairy laughed kindly. "Oh, gosh!" she giggled. "You fairies are gonna take a while to acclimatize, aren't you? There's no need for time here. Things happen when things happen. Sometimes things get done, and sometimes they don't. Either way the sun still shines."

Polly gulped. She was so used to being in control and prided herself on being organized and efficient. Being relaxed enough not to notice her watch was going to prove very hard.

"My name's Lola," said the skipper fairy as she ambled past them and began to untie the boat's ropes from the deck. "If you'd each be so kind as to fly carefully on to the boat we can see where the wind takes us."

Polly looked around frantically. Everything was still. There was no wind!

* * *

The boat trip proved to be one excursion none of the fairies would ever forget. With no breeze to blow them, the boat's patchwork sails stood motionless, so Lola gently guided the vessel with her enormous floppy wings.

It seemed to take for ever to go just a tiny distance, but somehow because the sky was so blue, the air so still and beautiful, and the birdsong so enchanting, it didn't seem to matter. When eventually they landed on a small rocky coastline, Polly was the only one who wasn't snoozing in the summer sun.

"I don't recognize this from my map," said Polly, looking at her book and then at the shoreline.

"No," said Lola slowly. "Can't say I recognize it either."

Polly looked aghast "You mean you've bought us to a place and you don't know where it is? We need to get to our hotel!"

"Oh, well," said Lola, with an unconcerned shrug. "I'm sure something will turn up."

Polly was as near as she had ever been to losing her temper. "Turn up!" she squealed in disbelief, waking the other fairies.

"Whatever is the matter?" asked Felicity, rubbing her sleepy eyes.

Just then two tiny fairies, no bigger than Felicity's rucksack, suddenly appeared, hovering above the patchwork sail of the boat.

Lola smiled. "Told you something would turn up!" she said, and winked at Polly.

* * *

The two tiny Bird Island fairies were called Twilla and Trill. They had been watching Lola's boat meandering its way for most of the afternoon, from their tiny hilltop home. Being so out of the way meant that visitors to Bird Island were very few and far between, and the boat's arrival was already the talk of their village.

"We'd be honoured it you'd stay with us," chirped Twilla musically.

Lola saw the uncertain look on Polly's face. "Nobody at the hotel is going to mind whether you turn up or not. I told you, people are a lot more relaxed out here!"

Trill nodded. "Our home isn't a hotel and it doesn't have a sea view, but it is right at the top of the mountain, where you'll be completely immersed in all the wonders Bird Island has to offer."

"It sounds amazing," said Felicity, delighted to make new friends. "We'd love to stay with you, thank you."

"You'll find the fairies in our village at the top of the hill very friendly," said Twilla.

"Aren't all the fairies on Bird Island friendly?" joked Holly, putting on her backpack ready for the long trek up the hill.

Trill looked awkwardly at Twilla, and Twilla tried desperately to change the subject.

Felicity looked quizzically at her new friends.

At last, after a long pause, Lola spoke. "Fairies at the top of the hill and fairies at the bottom of the hill don't mix, I'm afraid. It's always been that way."

Felicity was shocked. "How can you not be friends with every fairy?" she asked. Being the friendliest fairy in Little Blossoming, Felicity couldn't imagine not being friends with everyone she met.

Twilla's reply was quiet. "It's not that we're not friendly, it's just that the fairies at the bottom of the hill always ignore us, so we ignore them. There's no bad feeling, that's just how it is. Like Lola said, it's been like that for as long as anyone can remember."

* * *

The climb up the hill wasn't as long

as the fairy friends had feared. When they got to the top, dozens of village fairies were waiting to serve them with ice-cold drinks of rainbow juice.

"This is our nest," said Twilla. "If you look carefully there are dozens of nests in the trees in the village."

"I'd never have known they were here if you hadn't shown us," said Polly, squinting into the jungle.

"Not many fairies do know we're here," said Twilla. "We're certainly not in the guidebooks."

"How lucky we are!" thought Felicity, as she took a long sip of her rainbow juice and looked around at the hundreds of beautiful and exotic birds that were everywhere. Some birds flew high in the sky, braver species flew close to the fairies, and one even sat next to Felicity's bird,

Bertie Dishes, on her shoulder. Bertie was in bird heaven!

* * *

Over the next few days all six fairy friends agreed that it had been magical luck that had brought them to this place. The fairies in the village were the most generous they had ever met, and Twilla and Trill were perfect hosts.

"I've never felt so at home in a place that wasn't home," said Felicity as they were getting ready for bed one night.

"It's so relaxing here, and yet so exciting!" agreed Holly, remembering the flight they'd taken earlier that day. They'd swooped and swished high above the trees, with exotic lilac-lick birds circling around them.

Daisy was in her element. "I think

I've been shown every single native flower on the island," she said, leafing through her book.

"I can't wait for the annual Bird Island summer festival party!" said Winnie. "Twilla said they have music, fireworks, dancing and everyone decorates their crowns with feathers from their favourite bird!"

"It does sound fantastic," agreed Holly. "But I'm not looking forward to going home the day after."

"At least we have our trip to the beach tomorrow to look forward to," said Polly, pulling on her pyjamas.

"Hmmm," said Felicity thoughtfully. "It's a shame that Twilla and Trill don't feel they can come with us, because of the fairies at the bottom of the hill."

* * *

That night Felicity had the most amazing dream, and in the morning she knew she had to make it come true…

* * *

Bird Island cove was beautiful. It wasn't very far from where Lola should have brought the fairies originally. Polly gasped as she saw the magnificent hotel they had been going to stay in.

"This is so different to the top of the hill!" said Daisy as the friends flew in closer.

"It's not as natural as the top of the hill, but it still has a fairy-made beauty all of its own," observed Polly.

"I wonder if the fairies are as unfriendly as the fairies at the top of the hill think they are," said Felicity tentatively, preparing herself to be ignored.

* * *

But when Felicity, Holly, Polly, Daisy, Winnie and Kristen landed they couldn't have been more surprised.

"Hi there!" said a fairy, running up to greet them. "Welcome to Bird Island! Where are you all from?" she asked enthusiastically.

"We're from Little Blossoming," said Felicity, slightly taken aback.

"Wow!" said the lower-hill fairy. "That's a long way away! My name's Songella and I'm touched you've made the journey all the way here to visit our beautiful island. You're right on time for the big party tomorrow. Have you just arrived?"

Felicity looked around at her friends and nervously answered. "No, no. In fact, we've been here a week already, staying at the top of the hill."

Songella's face fell. "At the top of the hill?"

"Yes," said Felicity, her wings quivering in anticipation.

"We've had the best time!" added Polly quickly. "They've been so friendly."

The surprise on Songella's face was easy to see. "How strange," she said. "For some reason or other the fairies at the top of the hill have never been friendly to us. In fact, they just ignore us when we see them, so we ignore them too!"

Felicity couldn't believe what she was hearing!

"But the fairies at the top of the hill ignore you because they think that you don't want to be friends with them!" she burst out.

"What a silly misunderstanding!" said Songella. "Well, perhaps when you go back to stay with them tonight you can tell them that we're not

unfriendly at all... and today I'm going to prove it to you!"

* * *

Felicity, Holly, Polly, Daisy, Winnie, and Kristen had the most fun day of the entire holiday. They bounced over the waves on a rubber ring pulled by a super-fast speedboat, scuba-dived around the cove, and surfed the enormous white foamy waves that crashed on to the beach.

"I'm utterly exhausted!" said Polly when the fairies got back to their nest that evening.

"Me too!" said Daisy, snuggling under her duvet.

"Well, we had better get our beauty sleep if we want to look our best for the party tomorrow," said Holly.

"And with a little help from us, it will be the best celebration Bird Island has ever had," said Felicity, with a knowing smile.

* * *

All day preparations were made at the top of the hill. Fairies carefully stuck feathers to their crowns, baked cakes and transported musical instruments to a wonderful, wild clearing halfway down the hill. It had been the fantastic idea of one of the guests staying with Twilla and Trill to have it in that magical spot.

* * *

And all day at the bottom of the hill

preparations were equally productive. Fireworks were assembled, decorations were unpacked and party games chosen for their night-time venue halfway up the hill. A friend of Songella's had suggested holding the party somewhere different this year, and everyone agreed the clearing in the middle of the jungle was perfect!

* * *

With all the hustle and bustle going on, no one noticed that there were twice as many fairies than usual. All anyone noticed was that it was the most amazing party there had ever been, with twice the amount of festive food, twice the number of party games and twice the amount of fairy fun. Felicity made as many friends in one evening as she had on her entire holiday trip!

It was with calls from the crowds that, as honoured guests, Felicity and her friends were persuaded to say a few words before the fireworks ended the evening with a bang.

Felicity spoke on behalf of her friends. “Hello!” she said into the crackly microphone.

"I would just like to say a few words before our holiday sadly comes to an end," she said with a tear in her eye. "Holidays teach you a lot more than how to have fun flying with lilac-lick birds or scuba-diving around Bird Island coral. This holiday has taught all of us one of the most important things we shall ever remember. No matter how different we seem sometimes on the outside, we are all the same on the inside. That is why it makes me especially happy tonight to see fairies from the top and fairies from the bottom of this beautiful island celebrating together."

Suddenly the audience was awash with gasps, which one by one turned

into cheers. No one had even noticed that they had been partying with fairies they might have ignored on any other day.

Felicity gazed at her new friends with joy. "Thank you for the memories that we will cherish for ever, and for a perfect end to a perfect holiday."

Watch misunderstandings
magically disappear

when you communicate
with an open heart

Emma Thomson's *Felicity Wishes*®

After a freak fairy flood
ruins her home, Polly moves in
with Felicity Wishes in

Perfect Polly

Perfect Polly

Felicity Wishes' four closest friends were Holly, Polly, Daisy and Winnie. But it was Polly who was her best friend. They had known each other so long that neither of them could remember where and when they met. Felicity often thought that it was a very peculiar friendship, because she and Polly were so entirely different.

Felicity was carefree, silly and more

than a little messy. Polly, on the other hand, was clever, neat and impossibly perfect in almost everything she did. Felicity longed to be like Polly, although she wasn't sure Polly wanted to be like her!

* * *

"What are you up to?" Polly said to Felicity when her friend opened the door covered in paint. It was Sunday morning, and Polly had come round to see whether Felicity wanted to go out for a hot chocolate.

"Spur of the moment!" Felicity began. "I was sitting on the sofa last night just before I went to bed, wondering what my sitting room would look like if it was blue. Then I remembered I had a lovely blue crayon in the kitchen drawer."

"Tell me you didn't colour in your

sitting-room wall with crayon!" exclaimed Polly, aghast.

"Well, not exactly," said Felicity, showing her friend in. "I coloured in a small square, thought it looked horrid, and went to bed."

Polly frowned at Felicity's overall, dripping with bright-green paint.

"I'd forgotten all about it," continued Felicity, "until I walked into the sitting room when I got back from shopping. I tried to rub the crayon off, but it made such a mess that the only thing to do was paint over it, and all I had in the shed was this green, and it's a bit lumpy…" Felicity's voice trailed off.

"Oh, Felicity!" said Polly. She was well used to finding her friend in situations like this and immediately took charge. First she cleaned up the green footprints that trailed over most of the house, then, while Felicity made hot chocolate, Polly flew to Do-It-Together and picked up a large can of Sky Blue super-strength paint. They spent the whole afternoon and most of the evening painting, and by suppertime the room was entirely back to normal.

"You're perfect, Pol," said Felicity, settling down to cheese on toast in her newly painted sitting room.

"I know it sounds boring," began Polly, "but it really is much better sometimes to plan things in advance, instead of doing everything on the spur of the moment."

* * *

Every Sunday evening Polly wrote an intricate diary of what she had to do that week.

MONDAY

Make packed lunch,
meet Holly 8 a.m.

School all day.
Maths test in the afternoon.
Chemistry homework due.
After-school flying club.
Soup for supper.
Bed 9 p.m., read 30 mins
History of Little Blossoming.

TUESDAY

Make packed lunch,
meet Holly 8 a.m.

School all day.
English homework due.
Meet Felicity after school.
Sandwich for supper.
Bed 9 p.m., read 30 mins
History of Little Blossoming,
chapter 2

Polly opened the top drawer of her spotless chest of drawers, chose a fresh pair of pyjamas, had a bath and jumped in between the newly ironed sheets. It was her favourite time of the week, knowing that everything was ready, planned and accounted for. Polly's meticulous arrangements meant that she was never late for anything, never arrived anywhere unprepared and was always on time. She fell happily asleep to the patter of rain on the roof.

* * *

Holly looked at her watch: ten past eight. It was so unlike Polly to be late, especially on the day when every fairy in the School of Nine Wishes knew that there was an important maths test. And Polly always got top marks.

After trying Polly on her mobile phone and leaving a message, Holly decided to fly on and meet the others.

"It's not like her," said Daisy.

"Polly's planning to beat the school record in this test," said Winnie. "I know she's been working every morning before she comes to school."

"I couldn't do anything before school except sleep!" mused Felicity.

"What do you mean?" joked Holly. "Sometimes you don't even wake up before school. I'm not the only one who's heard you snore in assembly!"

"I'd love to be more like Polly," said Felicity dreamily.

"You wouldn't be you if you were Polly!" said Holly, hugging her friend.

* * *

When Polly didn't turn up at school that morning, Felicity decided to fly to her house at break-time to see if she could find out what had happened to her best friend. Felicity hadn't even reached Polly's house before she saw something that surprised her even more than Polly being late for school.

Polly lived in a valley next to a small pond. But where Polly's house should have been was a very large, very deep and very blue lake!

As Felicity flew nearer she could just make out the top storey and roof of Polly's house, peeping from under the lake.

Polly was flying waist-deep in water, dragging heavy buckets behind her.

"What in Fairy World?" called Felicity.

"A freak fairy flood!" said Polly, reaching the dry land further up the hill. "I don't know what time last night it happened, but when I woke up the whole of my downstairs and garden was submerged!"

"How awful!" said Felicity. "I hope no one was hurt."

"No, we were very lucky. Some other fairies have had their houses flooded too, but no one was injured. The water will drain away eventually, but what am I going to do in the meantime?" said Polly, with a lump in her throat.

Felicity didn't know what to say. It was usually Polly who took charge of catastrophes like this, but Polly herself never had catastrophes!

"I've phoned the fairy fire brigade," Polly said, reading her friend's thoughts, "but they said they're helping other fairies in Little Blossoming, and it may be some time before they can get here."

Felicity hugged her wet friend.

"Could you go and tell Fairy Godmother for me?" urged Polly, finally wriggling from the cuddle. "My mobile phone is waterlogged."

"I'll do better than that!" said Felicity, with a flash of inspiration. "I'll go and come back with as many fairies as I can, to help clear up this mess." And in a flutter Felicity had gone.

* * *

It took twelve fairies more than a day and a half to clear up the water that had drenched Polly's house. It had been easy to find offers of help when it meant getting out of the maths test!

After they'd finished, Felicity stayed with Polly to help tidy up.

"This is pointless," sobbed Polly as she picked up one of her homework books, only to see it fall away from her hand in a soggy lump. "Everything is ruined! This book was full of perfectly neat history homework. Ten out of ten all the way through. And now look at it!"

Felicity put her arm around Polly's shoulder. "Why don't you come back and stay at my house for a while until everything dries out?"

Polly wasn't keen. It was in her nature to get jobs done and to be in control. She knew that to be quite happy she would have to be back at the point she had been, so cosily, on Sunday evening.

Felicity sighed as Polly determinedly pulled out a hairdryer from under a pile of wet clothes, looked at it, and then at the enormous mess of damp things that surrounded them.

"I guess you're right," said Polly.

"It will be fun!" encouraged Felicity. But Polly wasn't so sure.

* * *

It only took one day of living with Felicity before Polly wasn't perfect any more.

Even though she'd been awake in plenty of time to get to school, it had taken her twice as long to get dressed. When Polly had moved in the night before, with her single suitcase of dry clothes, Felicity had tried to find room in her wardrobe. But the only space she discovered big enough for the case was on the floor. And it hadn't taken long before Polly's suitcase was buried under the bits and bobs that littered Felicity's room.

Even when Polly had found her suitcase, located the ironing board, got dressed and waited patiently by the front door, she could still hear Felicity's snores! And Polly couldn't bring herself to leave without her friend. Not when Felicity had been so kind to her.

* * *

The first week didn't go well. Polly found staying with Felicity increasingly frustrating, from the mess in the kitchen to her haphazard lifestyle.

"Have you ever thought of using a

diary?" suggested Polly, who had already been to the fairy stationer to replace her damp one.

"I had one once..." said Felicity. "It was more of a secret diary than an everyday diary. But I put it somewhere so secret that even I couldn't find it!"

"You've been very kind in letting me stay," ventured Polly. "But I'm afraid I have to be honest, for the sake of our friendship. I can't live the way that you do. My things won't be dry for at least another week, and I was wondering if I might help you be a little more organized in that time."

It was like sparkledust to Felicity's ears. She had always aspired to be more like her friend and here, at last, was her chance.

"Yes! Yes!" said Felicity, clapping

her hands. "When do we start?"

"Right now?" said Polly, glancing at the mess in the sitting room.

"Great," said Felicity, and they got stuck in straight away, cleaning, sorting and folding.

When Felicity climbed into bed that night she was snuggled between crisp clean sheets and wearing freshly ironed pyjamas.

"I could get used to this!" Felicity said to Bertie. Polly had insisted that he must sleep on his own bed, next to Felicity's, so he didn't leave feathers on the pillow. Bertie wasn't so sure this was a good idea.

* * *

As the second week progressed, however, it was now Felicity who found living with Polly increasingly difficult – from the constant tidying to the continual organizing of their lives. They rarely seemed to do anything on the spur of the moment.

Read the rest of

Emma Thomson's

Felicity Wishes®

Perfect Polly

to find out whether Felicity and Polly's friendship will last.

If you enjoyed this book, why not try another of these fantastic story collections?

8

Friends Forever

7

Sensational Secrets

9

Happy Hobbies

Wand Wishes

10

Party Pickle

12

Dancing Dreams

14
Emma Thomson's
Felicity Wishes
Fashion Fiasco
and other stories
Fashion Fiasco
13
Emma Thomson's
Felicity Wishes
Spooky Sleepover
and other stories
Spooky Sleepover
15
Felicity Wishes
Pink Paradise
and other stories
Pink Paradise
17
Felicity Wishes
Dreamy Daisy
and other stories
Dreamy Daisy
16
Felicity Wishes
Spectacular Skies
and other stories
Spectacular Skies
18
Felicity Wishes
Perfect Polly
and other stories
Perfect Polly

20
felicity Wishes
Holly's Hideaway
and other stories
Holly's Hideaway
19
felicity Wishes
Winnie's Wonderland
and other stories
Winnie's Wonderland
21
felicity Wishes
Fairy Fun
and other stories
Fairy Fun
Look out for these three special editions
Summer Sunshine
Christmas Calamity
felicity Wishes
Christmas Calamity
and other stories
felicity Wishes
Summer Sunshine
and other stories
Winter Wishes
felicity Wishes
Winter Wishes
and other stories

SEE YOUR FRIENDSHIP LETTER HERE!

Write in and tell us all about your best friend, and you could see your letter published in one of the Felicity Wishes' books.

Please send in your letter, including your name and age with a stamped self-addressed envelope to:

Felicity Wishes Friendship Competition

Hodder Children's Books, 338 Euston Road, London NW1 3BH

Australian readers should write to...

Hachette Children's Books

Level 17/207 Kent Street, Sydney, NSW 2000, Australia

New Zealand readers should write to...

Hachette Children's Books

PO Box 100-749 North Shore Mail Centre, Auckland, New Zealand

Closing date is 31 December 2007

ALL ENTRIES MUST BE SIGNED BY A PARENT OR GUARDIAN.
TO BE ELIGIBLE ENTRANTS MUST BE UNDER 13 YEARS.

For full terms and conditions visit www.felicitywishes.net/terms

Dear felicity

My friend is called rose.
She is My friend because She is
nice and She is always happy
and Smiling and we Somtime
give eathother piggy back's
and we can't Stop laghing
I play with her all the time.
She has a very Cheeky Smile
and is alway's laghing
I think She will be glad
that I am writing about her.

Lots of Love from Charlotte
xxx

WIN FELICITY WISHES PRIZES!

From January 2006, there will be a Felicity Wishes fiction book publishing each month (in Australia and New Zealand publishing from April 2006) with a different sticker on each cover. Collect all twelve stickers and stick them on the collectors' card which you'll find in Dancing Dreams or download from www.felicitywishes.net

Send in your completed card to the relevant address below and you'll be entered into a grand prize draw to receive a Felicity Wishes prize.*

Felicity Wishes Collectors' Competition

Hodder Children's Books, 338 Euston Road, London NW1 3BH

Australian readers should write to...

Hachette Children's Books

Level 17/207 Kent Street, Sydney, NSW 2000, Australia

New Zealand readers should write to...

Hachette Children's Books

PO Box 100-749 North Shore Mail Centre, Auckland, New Zealand

*A draw to pick 50 winners each month will take place from January 2007 – 30th June 2007.

For full terms and conditions visit www.felicitywishes.net/terms

WOULD YOU LIKE TO BE A FRIEND OF FELICITY?

Felicity Wishes has her very own website, filled with lots of sparkly fairy fun and information about Felicity Wishes and all her fairy friends.

Just visit:

www.felicitywishes.net

to find out all about Felicity's books, sign up to competitions, quizzes and special offers.

And if you want to show how much you love your friends, you can even send them a Felicity e-card for free. It will truly brighten up their day!